To C. J.
from O.C —

Sincerely
Olga Classi

June 11, 1990

ORLANDA

&

The Contest of Thieves

ORLANDA

&

The Contest of Thieves

story by Olga Cossi
illustrations by Tom Sarmo

Bookmakers Guild, Inc.

Published in 1989 in the United States of America by
Bookmakers Guild, Inc.
9655 West Colfax Avenue
Lakewood, Colorado 80215

Printed and bound in the United States of America

Hardcover: ISBN 0-917665-32-5

Library of Congress Cataloging-in-Publication Data

Cossi, Olga.
   Orlanda & the contest of thieves / by Olga Cossi; illustrated by Tom Sarmo.
     pp. 32
   Summary: The orphan Orlanda enters a contest sponsored by the Lord Mayor of Naples and seeks to prove that she is the best at stealing the impossible.
    ISBN 0-917665-32-5 : $14.95
    [1. Folklore—Italy.] I. Sarmo, Tom, ill. II. Title.
III. Title: Orlanda and the contest of thieves.
PZ8.1.C788Or   1989
398.2'0945—dc20

89-15107
CIP
AC

  Thank you to Alfred F. Alberico, professor emeritus at San Francisco State University, for the researched information on Mt. Faito and the short-toed eagle.

Other Books for Young People
by Olga Cossi

Robin Deer
Fire Mate
Gus the Bus
The Magic Box
The Great Getaway
Ice Babies
The Wonderful, Wonder-Full Donkey

To Papa,
the storyteller

Chapter One

On the streets of Naples in southern Italy lived a ragged wisp of a girl named Orlanda. She was born in the faraway village of Porcari and taken to Naples when she was an infant. There she was abandoned in a narrow alley on the wrong side of the piazza and left to make her own way through life as best she could.

Orlanda shared the dark corners she called home with a pack of grizzled alley cats. From them she learned how to slink slightly through the city and prowl all night without being seen or heard.

By the time she was five years old, Orlanda could steal food from the street vendors without getting caught. By the time she was eleven, she was a crafty pickpocket with a cache of wallets and a bag of stolen jewelry to her credit.

One day in the heart of the city, a crowd of people gathered to hear an official announcement by the Lord Mayor of Naples. Orlanda crouched in the shadows of a side street to hear what he had to say.

"Something must be done about it!" shouted the Lord Mayor, his face as red as his necktie. "Naples has become the Thief Capital of the World! Something must be done to rid our streets of thieves!"

"Bravo!" shouted the people.

"Bravo!" shouted the city council.

"Down with the Lord Mayor!" muttered Orlanda under her breath.

Zarmida, the Lord Mayor's wife, got up then and stood beside her husband. She knew that to catch a thief you must be clever — very, very clever. To catch a horde of thieves, you must have a Plan.

"I have a Plan!" Zarmida announced with a wink at the crowd.

"Let us hold a Contest of Thieves," she began. "Let every thief who lives on our streets try to steal the most impossible thing he or she can think of. Those who succeed will compete against each other until only one winner remains. Those who fail will be banished from the city and can never, NEVER return!"

"Tell us more! Tell us more!" begged the crowd.

"Tell us more!" echoed Orlanda, beginning to like the idea.

Zarmida winked again as she continued. "The winner will be named Champion Thief of the World. As a special prize, he or she will be given a seat on the city council and made the Street Chief of Naples, whose official duty will be to keep the streets of our city free from thieves once and for all!"

"Oh, to become World Champion and rule the streets of Naples!" thought Orlanda. "If only I win the contest I could live in a house on the right side of the piazza! I could sleep in a bed and eat at a table! As Street Chief of Naples, I would never let another thief set foot inside the city gates!"

"What if you fail?" asked her conscience.

"Fail?" thought Orlanda. "Never! Besides, what have I got to lose? Here is my chance to be on the side of the law at last, instead of against it!"

3

"But who are you to compete against the master thieves of Naples?" continued her conscience. "Doesn't this city have the slickest, greediest, cleverest gathering of pickpockets and fingersmiths, housebreakers and safecrackers, highway robbers and hijackers to be found anywhere in the world?"

Orlanda looked at her reflection in a shop window. She was dressed in a gown of faded purple spangles, as tattered as the hair on her head. Around her shoulders hung a satin cape, worn thin and smooth as her slender fingers. And on her feet were the barest blue sandals, as light and soft as her footsteps.

"I may not look like much," she admitted, standing as tall as she could. "But when it comes to doing the impossible, I am as good as the best!"

Orlanda spoke to her reflection in the window. "You are Orlanda of Porcari!" she declared. "By the end of the contest you will be Orlanda of Naples, Street Chief of the city and Champion Thief of the World!"

Chapter Two

The Contest of Thieves began that very hour. Robbers and pillagers by the hundreds hurried out of their hiding places, eager to show off in front of the crowd. There were old thieves and young ones, male thieves and females, some dressed like beggars and some dressed like kings. Each one was so anxious to win the contest that not once did a single thief stop to consider the rule that those who failed would be banished from the city and could never, NEVER return.

Orlanda knew there was no time to lose. The competition would be fast and furious. There would be bold feats of cunning that no one had ever seen before, not even the crustiest thieves. She must think, *think*, THINK!

She crouched in her dark corner and watched the first contestant step forth. His name was Aldo the Elder. He was the oldest thief in Naples. He was so old he could remember when the city was ruled by a French king.

"I will steal the gold key to our city!" he boasted. It was the most impossible thing he could think of.

The key was kept in a display case in front of the City Hall guarded day and night by armed sentries. Aldo dressed up like a flower vendor and pushed his cart as close to the case as he dared.

The beautiful colors of the bouquets caught the eye of the sentry on duty. The flowers reminded him of his sweet Filomena and the tryst he would have with her that night. Ah, she would fall madly in love with the flowers, and with him, if he brought her a bouquet. But which nosegay would she like best? Which posies would make her melt in his arms?

While the sentry fondled the flowers, dreaming of Filomena and trying to decide the right bouquet to choose, Aldo frantically fingered the lock on the display case, trying to find the right combination.

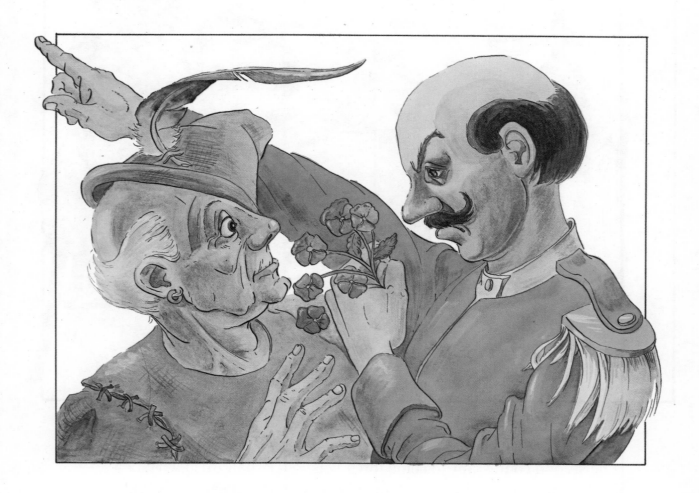

At the very moment that the door to the display case sprang open, an angry bee buzzed by the sentry's bald head and then stung him with a passion.

"Aaaaayiiiii!" bellowed the sentry, coming to his senses and catching Aldo with the key in his hand.

"So, you were trying to make a fool of me with flowers!" he shouted, holding his head to keep it from swelling. "Throw him and his cart out of the city gates!" he ordered.

And that was the end of Aldo.

The second contestant to come forth was Peter the Putrid. Orlanda knew him well. He had so little honor that even the alley cats would not go near him.

"I will make off with the Bishop's false teeth — mind you, while he is eating his noon meal of pasta with pesto!" he boasted. It was the most preposterous thing he could think of.

Peter waited until the Bishop was busy filling his glass with red wine before he slithered on his belly into the dining room. He waited until the Bishop struggled to tie a linen napkin under his three chins before he snaked his way across the floor. He waited until the chef himself carried in the plate of steaming pasta before he crept under the Bishop's table.

Before Peter could reach up and snatch the false teeth in mid-bite, the Bishop began to pepper his pasta. Alas, the pepper was too much for the poor thief's nose. It twitched and it tickled and finally it EXPLODED!

"Ahhhhhhhhh...choooooooooo!"

And out the city gates went another loser.

Next came Greggorio the Greedy. Orlanda knew him, too. He was so greedy that he had even tried to steal from her.

"I will enter the cage of the hungriest lion in the city zoo and steal a bone from under his very paws!" he bragged.

Now, everyone knew how impossible that was!

Greggorio disguised himself as a log by wrapping his body from head to toe in the bark of a newly fallen tree. Then he bribed the zookeeper to open the gate of the lion's cage just enough so he could roll inside.

Slowly, slowly, Greggorio made his advance. He rolled closer to the lion and the juicy rib bone clutched in the beast's thick paws. He rolled within six feet of those paws. Then he rolled within an arm's length of them.

Without moving a leaf of his disguise, Greggorio buried one finger in the dirt like an inchworm and dug straight toward the bone. Precisely as his fingernail hooked the rib to draw it into his grasp, the lion gave a hungry roar. Unfortunately, Greggorio had not taken the time to eat breakfast that morning, and his stomach growled back!

Needless to say, that was one thief who did not have to be banished from the city!

At last it was Orlanda's turn. She had some special tricks up her ragged sleeves, and now was the time to try them.

"I will enter the summer palace of the Prince of Persia and make off with his favorite cross-eyed kitten!" she declared.

"What is so incredible about that?" snarled one of the other thieves.

"I will do this while the pampered pet is taking a nap on the Prince's lap!" Orlanda added.

With that she took off, making her way toward the secret passage into the Prince's private chambers that only she and the alley cats knew.

Orlanda was so thin that the Prince's porters did not see her when she slipped past them like a purple shadow. Her footsteps were so light that the Prince's ears did not hear a sound as she tiptoed to his side. Her movements were so swift and sure that before the cross-eyed kitten could stop purring, she had lifted it by the nape of the neck and was on her way back to the city square.

"I cannot believe that this...this...*child* is our first winner!" sputtered the Lord Mayor as his wife petted the Persian kitten.

But it was true. Orlanda had indeed succeeded in her first attempt to win the contest. Now she must wait to see how many other thieves succeeded as well.

Chapter Three

Swarms of thieves stole through the streets of Naples, trying ever more daring deeds to win the Contest of Thieves according to Zarmida's Plan. One outrageous attempt followed another as poachers and marauders from every quarter of the city put their most absurd schemes into action. Their brains scanned every impulse that came into their heads, trying to devise a feat no one else had imagined.

One by one, the thieves came forth to make a boast and try to carry it out.

One by one they failed. One by one, those who failed were forced to leave the city and never, NEVER return.

After five days, only five thieves were left in the entire city of Naples. Orlanda's heart beat faster as the Lord Mayor read their names.

"The five semifinalists are: Useless Ulysses, Niki the Knife, Wily Willy, Abdul of Alexandria, and Orlanda of Porcari!"

"Our semifinal contest will begin at dawn tomorrow," announced Zarmida.

Orlanda did not sleep all night. She prowled the streets of Naples with the pack of alley cats at her heels. Her sharp eyes looked this way and that, searching for something so remarkable that no one else would even think of trying to steal it.

When the sun came up on the sixth day, Orlanda knew exactly what she would do. She joined the crowd that gathered to hear the official announcement.

"Let the semifinal contest begin!" shouted Zarmida.

"Let the semifinal contest begin!" echoed the crowd.

Orlanda smiled to herself as the four other thieves set forth, their fingers twitching nervously. With each passing hour, they became more rash and reckless, their deeds more daring, their failures more final.

By late afternoon, only two thieves remained within the city gates of Naples.

One was Abdul of Alexandria.

The other was Orlanda of Porcari.

Abdul had succeeded in the unheard-of attempt to steal the wig off the head of the soprano as she sang a solo in the Opera House before an audience of six thousand people. Abdul bowed as he presented the wig to the Lord Mayor and the city council.

The crowd cheered and cheered. "Bravo! Bravo!"

They knew that Abdul was a thief. They knew that he had stolen from them many times. But there was nothing they liked better than a contest, and here was a winner! They clapped their hands and tossed caps and bonnets into the air.

But Orlanda had matched Abdul's daring, deed for deed. She had succeeded in stealing the coat of arms off the royal coach of the Queen of England while the Queen herself was riding in it on her way to the semifinal contest. Orlanda bowed as she presented the coat of arms to the Lord Mayor and the city council.

"Who is this Orlanda of Porcari?" everyone asked.

"Doesn't she live on one of the narrowest streets on the wrong side of the piazza?"

"Is she old enough to be a thief?"

"How can she hope to compete against the likes of Abdul?"

Still, the crowd had to admit she was clever. Very clever. They cheered "Bravo! Bravo!" as they clapped their hands and tossed caps and bonnets into the air.

"We will now commence the final event of the contest!" cried Zarmida. "Which of these two winners will become World Champion and Street Chief of our city?

"Abdul of Alexandria...or Orlanda of Porcari?"

Chapter Four

There was excitement in the air as Orlanda stood beside Abdul and listened to Zarmida explain the final details of her Plan.

"On the top of Mount Faito, not far from our city, grows one of the tallest trees in Italy," she began. "On the highest branch of that tree there is a large straw nest. Inside the nest there are three delicate eggs. And sitting on the eggs is a short-toed eagle. This beautiful bird has fiery eyes that never close. She has a razor-sharp beak that frightens away the most fearless hawk. And she has long, thin claws — strong enough to kill anything that tries to go near her nest."

Zarmida turned to Abdul and Orlanda. "Whoever can bring back an egg from the nest on the highest branch of the tallest tree on the top of Mount Faito without alarming the short-toed eagle will be declared winner of the final contest!"

"Unless," she added, raising her hand, "UNLESS either contestant can think of a feat more clever and daring than that!"

Immediately Abdul swaggered forth. He was wearing his pearl-button shoes and a pair of splendid gold braid suspenders he had stolen at the Opera House that morning. He was sure he could outwit both the short-toed eagle and this ragged wisp of a girl named Orlanda. Had he not entered the underground vault of the City

Treasury and made off with one of the bars of pure gold while the Treasurer himself was counting them to make sure they were all there?

Abdul turned his back on Orlanda and spoke in a loud voice. "My opponent is only a child. I will go first and save her the trouble of trying!"

Orlanda said nothing. She knew Abdul was a master of his craft. She knew her clothes were not as splendid as his. But she had done some things that even Abdul had not attempted. Had she not found a way into the stone cellar where the Lord Mayor kept his favorite sausage and made off with a string of the spicy salsiccia intended for his official mouth alone? Had she not removed the imperial ring off the Rajah's hand while the visiting monarch was stroking the head of his faithful tiger?

Orlanda had proved many times that she had a mind and wits of her own. She must use them now as never before. She quickly agreed to let Abdul go first. Meanwhile, she would think, *think,* THINK!

Orlanda followed the crowd that followed the Lord Mayor, his wife, and the city council who followed Abdul to the top of Mount Faito. There the final contest began.

As softly as a sea breeze whispers through swaying branches, Abdul started up the tree. He slithered up the trunk inch by inch, centimeter by centimeter.

At last, he reached the highest branch. Now he held his breath, lest the short-toed eagle hear him and snap off his head with her claws!

Abdul's hand was lighter than a feather as it moved slowly toward the nest.

More quietly than the blink of a fox's eyelash, his nimble fingers curled inside the straw.

More smoothly than a silken moth unfolds its wings, his fingertips closed around the egg.

    With less fuss than a poppy opening its petals, he slipped the egg from the nest.

    Still holding his breath, Abdul cradled the stolen egg in his palm and slid down the tree trunk. His eyes gleamed with pride as his feet touched the ground.

    Abdul turned to face the Lord Mayor and the city council. He couldn't wait to present them with the stolen egg and accept the honor of becoming Champion Thief of the World, and, of course, the special prize of an official seat on the city council as Street Chief of Naples.

But something was wrong. The people were laughing instead of cheering. They were laughing so hard that tears were streaming down their cheeks. Some of them were rolling on the ground, holding their sides. And they were laughing at *him!*

"Why are you laughing instead of cheering?" gasped Abdul. "And why is the Lord Mayor presenting the title and the special prize to Orlanda instead of to me?"

"Look at yourself!" laughed Zarmida, tittering at the top of her voice. "Just look at what this mere wisp of a girl has done to you!"

Abdul looked. Suddenly he saw that his pearl-button shoes were missing!

Then he saw that the pair of splendid gold braid suspenders he had stolen from the Opera House that morning were missing!

What's more, HIS PANTS WERE MISSING!

For while Abdul had slithered up the tree to steal the egg from the short-toed eagle's nest without alarming her, Orlanda had thought of a feat even more clever and daring than that.

She had shadowed Abdul up the tree and without so much as a hush of sound, removed the shoes off his feet, the suspenders off his pants, and finally the pants themselves! And she had presented them to Zarmida before Abdul's bare feet had touched the ground.

So it was that Zarmida's Plan for a Contest of Thieves succeeded. The hordes of thieves were gone from the city streets.

Orlanda of Porcari became Orlanda of Naples, Champion Thief of the World and Street Chief of Naples. She moved into a big house on the right side of the piazza, where she slept in a soft bed and ate at a table full of food. And as long as she lived, she never let another thief set foot inside the city gates.

P.S. Are you wondering what happened to Abdul? He did succeed in stealing the short-toed eagle's egg, you remember. Well, at the last minute he was not banished from the city. Instead, Zarmida and the city council voted to make him Orlanda's deputy. For in a city as worldly as Naples, even the Street Chief needs an assistant.